Tiggy and the Flying Fish

For my daughter Malou and her Grandpa in the Sky x

Copyright

Tiggy the Salty Sea Dog

Published:December 2022

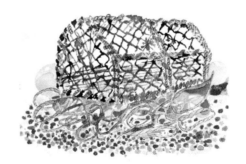

Tiggy and the Flying Fish

Written by Barney Clarke
Illustrated by Sam Scott

Seaside stories from the Kent Coast

It was another beautiful, sunny, spring morning in Hythe with clear blue skies, seagulls squawking and the faint sound of soft lapping waves on the beachfront behind Cinque Ports Avenue.

"Come on Tig, Tig, race you to the beach!" shouted Jake.

Excitedly, the boy and his faithful cockapoo ran down the narrow pathway, passing old fences with rickety gates and bright patches of wild flowers, then out onto the entrance to Fisherman's Beach.

The beach was busy today!

Tiggy bounded joyfully through the crowds outside the Lazy Shack Cafe
and headed straight towards the fishing boats.

"Slow down," called Jake as he sprinted hard
to keep up with her.

She whizzed through the maze of
old black fishing huts...

scrambled under piles of tangled netting...

jumped over lobster pots...

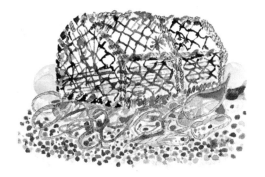

And eventually skidded to a halt staring out over
Fisherman's Beach searching for Big Barry's boat.

All the fishermen's boats were in for the day, there was...

Becky Jane, the biggest boat, painted in blue and white.

Francis B, the fastest boat, painted in navy blue and grey.

And Big Barry's boat, Mizpah 11, the newest boat, painted in black and white.

Tiggy dashed out to find Big Barry for a 'tremendous Tiggy tummy tickle!'

Tiggy and Jake explored further along the beach
the army ranges where there were two old army forts, Martello towers,
that looked a lot like giant sandcastles.

Each time they walked along the track past one of the large
range numbers Jake threw a pebble for Tiggy to find,
counting aloud...

Suddenly Tiggy stopped, raised a front paw and pointed her nose.

She could hear something!

Tiggy padded over to a young girl sitting crossed-legged on the sand and humming quietly, as she carefully tried to untangle the strings of a kite.

"Hello," Jake called down, "would you like some help with that?"
She looked up shyly and, with a relieved smile, replied, "Hello, yes please, that would be very kind. I'm Malou, what's your name?"

"Hi, I'm Jake and this is Tiggy."

Tiggy wagged her tail - she loved making new friends.

The three beach buddies looked at the tangled string and together they came up with a plan...
Firstly, Tiggy scampered down the beachfront with the kite in her mouth while Malou and Jake held the handle.

Secondly, they carefully twisted, turned, looped and pulled the string and the kite.

Until finally the strings lay neatly lined up along the beach, ready to launch the kite.

"Right, let's fly this thing!" announced Jake.
"Hooray!" cheered Malou.

Woof, Woof barked Tiggy, wagging her tail excitedly as she sped around
the kite in circles, spraying sand behind her.

"Tiggy, let's swap ends, you hold the handle and we will each hold a corner
of the kite. Then on the count of three we will throw it as high as we can
and Tig, you run as fast as you can!"

Tiggy darted across the sand, the string went tight, the kite bounced,
bumped and lifted.

Up, Up, Up And..............

AWAY!

The kite soared high into the sky, with its
tail scales flapping and shimmering in the sunlight.

Jake and Tiggy realised at that moment that the
kite was in the shape of a flying fish!
A magical Rainbow Fish of dazzling colour.

Malou's face lit up with a beautiful smile
from ear to ear.

"It's magnificent!" she shouted.
"Thank you, thank you."

Malou skipped with joy as she guided the kite,
fluttering and floating gracefully through the sky above.

Malou then gave Jake a turn. He tugged hard on the line and with a loud
'Whoosh" and "Swoosh" the kite zoomed and zigged and zagged and then
dipped and dived
like a giant serpent
leaping out of the
sea.

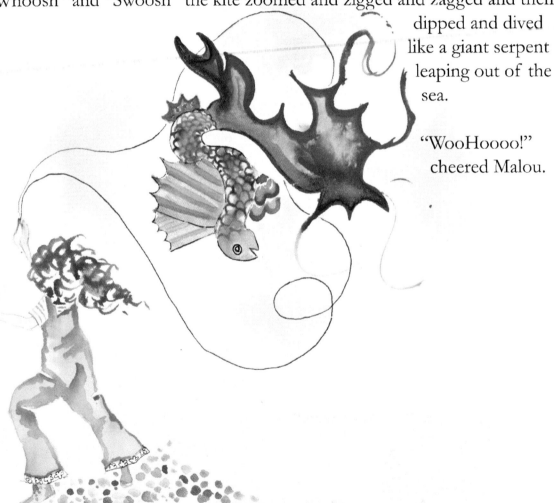

"WooHoooo!"
cheered Malou.

15

After what seemed like hours of fun the sun began to set.
"Sorry, but it is time to go Tig," said Jake,
sadly passing the kite back to Malou.
"Lovely to meet you! Maybe we will bring our kite next time
to show it to you.
We have one that is red dragon-shaped."

"Thank you and goodbye!' said Malou cheerfully,
giving her new doggy friend a 'tremendous Tiggy tummy tickle'.

As they walked home past the Lazy Shack Cafe,
families were pointing and smiling at the flying fish. Jake stopped to wave
back to Malou, and Tiggy gave a short friendly "Woof," goodbye.

Back at home on the sofa Tiggy and Jake sat side by side, dreaming of the next windy day and what other kites they may see in the skies above Hythe!

Maybe a Space Rocket

Maybe a Dinosaur

Maybe a Pirate Ship

Maybe a ....

Tiggy Challenge!

Can you sketch your own Fantastic Flying Fish kite on the next page?

Don't forget to add the:

- Fins
- Scales
- Tail
- Rainbow colours

Printed in Poland
by Amazon Fulfillment
Poland Sp. z o.o., Wrocław

17957819R00016